HORROR STORIES SET IN EARLY AMERICA, VOLUME TWO

H. Rad Bethlen

Rooster & Raven

Library of Congress Control Number: 2024948712

For the Daughters of Zeus and Mnemosyne

Author Statement Concerning Artificial Intelligence

The way I write consist of several phases.

1. Idea generation.
2. Research.
3. Story development.
4. Outlining.
5. Writing the rough draft.
6. Editing and rewriting.
7. Editing and polishing.
8. Copy editing.

I will *occasionally* use AI during the research phase if I can't locate some bit of information on my own—but I try to locate it on my own first.

I will *occasionally* use AI during the story's development if I get stuck on something—but I try to resolve my own story issues first.

I *intentionally* use AI during the copy editing phase as a stand-in for a copy editor, which I can't afford to pay for yet which I don't want to go without.

A copy editor is the last set of eyes to look at a manuscript to check for grammar, usage, spelling, and punctuation mistakes. I ask the AI copy editor to make suggestions on corrections. I evaluate those suggestions. If I agree, I make the changes.

I don't use AI for anything else.

Be comforted that these stories were written by a human being for other human beings.

H. Rad Bethlen

Excerpted from **California**. In 1776 Juan Bautista de Anza founded San Francisco. Already Father Junípero Serra and other Franciscans had established a string of missions.... The early colonist, called the Californios, lived a fairly easy pastoral life. They were not much molested by the central government of New Spain or later of Mexico, but they did indulge in strenuous local politics and in quarrels with their governors, such as Juan Bautista Alvarado. Many of the Indians were gathered about the missions, but when these were secularized under the Mexican republic (1833-34) the Indians were dispersed and victimized.

- The Columbia Encyclopedia

Serra, Junípero, 1713-84, Spanish Franciscan missionary in North America, b. Majorca. His name was originally Miguel José Serra, and Junípero was his name in religion. For 15 years he taught philosophy in the college of Palma. In 1749 he was sent to America with Francisco Palou, his lifelong friend and biographer, and proceeded to Mexico City, where he taught briefly at the College of San Fernando.

For three years he worked successfully among the Indians of the Sierra Gorda, then returned to Mexico City for seven more years, working half of each year in the surrounding villages. His passionate preaching and stern asceticism won him a large and respectful following. It was at this time that his self-mortification began and that legends began to grow up about him.

In 1769 Serra went with the second expedition to California, which was commanded by Gaspar de Portolá. When the party reached San Diego, Serra remained to found (1769) the mission there, while most of the rest of the party went on in search of the harbor of Monterey. When they returned unsuccessful, Serra was one of those responsible for the sending of a second expedition, which he accompanied.

- The Columbia Encyclopedia

This morning Archbishop Montoro delivered the sermon. Forgive me, Lord, I think him a villain. This is but a morsel of the poison he spewed upon us like so much vomit.

"Choose your own path," he shouted, "and you incur the wrath of the Devil." Over and over he said, "Listen to what the Church instructs! God has chosen Mother Church to point out what is right thinking and that which is not!"

I ask you, Lord, if there is truth to the Archbishop's message, why have you given me a mind of my own?

"Brother."

"Archbishop. Father."

The Franciscan monk, Gonçalo Romero, stood in the small office, head bowed, hands folded before him. Archbishop Segovia Montoro sat behind the desk. Father Adulfo Vivar stood.

The Archbishop rolled the golden cross he wore around his neck between his thumb and forefinger. His black hair fell across his forehead. He was young to be an archbishop, being only twenty-nine. Father Vivar was twice his age. Gonçalo was past forty and not well. He had faced many obstacles. They had taken their toll. Many of these difficulties were placed before him by the

Archbishop. This was only the second time they had met, despite their long history.

"How goes your writing?" asked Montoro, dropping the cross against his chest. Their eyes met. Gonçalo looked down and remained mute. "No more novels?"

"Archbishop?" asked Gonçalo.

"Do you think I've forgotten?" asked the Archbishop, rising. He stepped to the side and held the back of the chair, motioning with his other hand for Father Vivar to sit, as it was his chair.

"Thank you, Archbishop."

Montoro came around the desk and began a rude inspection, his eyes roving over Gonçalo, his brow knotted and his lips pressed together, the ends turned down. He reached out and stuck his finger into a hole in the rough fabric of Gonçalo's robe. He said nothing but passed behind. He came around, turned to face Gonçalo, and spoke. "But you *have* been writing."

Again Gonçalo looked. When their eyes met, Montoro's narrowed.

"You applied to a different order, yes? The Jesuits," he turned to Father Vivar. "They would not have him." He turned back to Gonçalo. "Of course, I gave them *my* opinion."

"You—" growled Gonçalo.

Montoro tilted his head. Gonçalo fell silent. Montoro continued. "You wrote—His Holiness. You wrote—the King. Tsk tsk." Montoro wagged a finger. "Do you believe these men have time for you? You are not fit to be a flyspeck on the hem of the king's robe." Father Vivar cleared his throat but the Archbishop ignored the censure. "After that filth you published—"

"It was not filth!"

"Brother Romero!" snapped Father Vivar. "Remember to whom you are speaking. I will not tolerate —"

Archbishop Montoro raised a hand. Father Vivar fell silent. "Do go on, Brother. Eh? Nothing more? I would like to know how you could defend a novel such as that. Of course, it's gone—every copy," he motioned as if dropping something, "into the fire."

Montoro stepped to the side of the desk and bent, placing his hands palms down on the dark wood. He looked from the sides of his eyes at Gonçalo then turned to Father Vivar.

"Of course, we could not allow him to continue his professorship." He stood and began to round the desk, pausing behind Father Vivar. He placed both hands on the top of Vivar's chair. "The new world, yes?" He smiled. "Do you miss the city, Gonçalo? Do you miss the stimulating intellectual milieu?" His smile faded. "Do these illiterate natives spur you to more novel writing?" He smirked. "No, I should think not."

"Archbishop, if I have offended you—"

"This has nothing to do with me!" Montoro gripped the chair with one hand, waving the other. "We, each of us, speaks for Mother Church. We are not at liberty to write and publish filth in her name. No!" He pointed at Gonçalo. "Hold your tongue!" Montoro relaxed his grip. He took a deep breath, released the chair, turned, head bowed, hands clasped behind his back, and continued around the desk, stopping at the edge. He looked up at Gonçalo. "I saw the look on your face this morning. I could read your thoughts. You despise me."

"Archbishop," said Father Vivar, "forgive me, but this conversation—"

Montoro did not look away from Gonçalo when he spoke, speaking over Father Vivar. "Junípero Serra, now there was a saint in the making. A much better man than *you*." Montoro's eyes moved over Gonçalo. "He had the grace and wisdom to disappear into the hinterlands." Montoro laughed. "How many missions did he found? Eh? A dozen? Such work leaves no time for novel writing—or letter writing."

He stood, gazing at Gonçalo. After a moment he turned to Father Vivar. He reached into his robe and pulled out a folded parchment, wrapped in scarlet ribbon, sealed with wax. He tossed the packet onto the desk. "Orders from Rome." He looked sidelong at Gonçalo. "You are to go to California, to Serra's missions. They have been neglected."

"But—" spat out Gonçalo.

"Archbishop," said Father Vivar. "The native peoples have—"

Montoro waved away Father Vivar's concerns. "I leave tomorrow. There is much I must do in Spain. There is much you," he smiled at Gonçalo, "must do in California."

That bastard! Forgive me, Lord. How have I made such an enemy as he? How can he act as he does? Doesn't he know You watch him inflict misery on others? First he denied me my novel. I do not even have my original. He had the pages taken from my cell when I was four days at fast in that miserable pit. Four days of water only, on my knees, begging forgiveness for a sin I knew was not a sin. Why? Had I offended the Church? I had I offended You?

Then he denied me my professorship. I loved the university! I loved to teach! I should be a Jesuit! I begged but no, he gave his *opinion. Next he arranged I be sent to the new world, to this primitive, violent land. Still, that was not enough. Orders from Rome? Orders from his own pen! To California! To Serra's missions! Do they still exist? Does he mean me to be killed? And what of my health? Will I survive such a—*

Forgive me. I show a lack of faith. He is Archbishop, yes, but he is just a man. You are Lord. You could not want me dead by savage hands. You will fortify my heart, my courage.

Forgive me. I will go.

The pony they gave me is delicate. This rocky, hilly terrain upsets her. She pauses to gauge every steep decline then looks over her shoulder at me, either doubting my wisdom or begging my mercy. I sympathize.

There are missionaries who learn to sleep under the stars with a crooked arm for a pillow. They find glory in the passing clouds. Praise them. Then there are men like me, who are better suited to gardens, plazas, libraries, cafes. I did not confuse myself between the one and the other. Nor did the Archbishop. He knew.

We came upon the southern most of Serra's missions. It was a simple square of mud brick, plastered white. A few desultory homes bunch together like frightened hens, clinging to the slope of a rocky, scrub-grassed hill. The locals stared at us as if we were apparitions. When we began to unload barrels of sugar and spice, casks of wine, and so forth they broke down in tears.

There were many natives milling about. They carry armfuls of pelts, worked leather goods, and their gaudy beads. They attempt to trade. Indeed, the mission is little more to them than a trading post. Didn't Christ upset the tables of the money changers? Where is the parish priest? Died, they told me, and took me to his grave. When I asked how, they shrugged their shoulders. Was he a man for libraries and cafes?

I baptized the young, spoke at the graves of the departed, heard the confession of every inhabitant, and gave a sermon—after clearing the cobwebs from Serra's mission. They have been neglected? Abandoned is more apt. I tasked an energetic youth to upkeep the mission and we moved on.

Another mission, same as before.

Another — same.

My pony is fed up with me. My hips ache. My entire butt is an aggravated bruise. I can find no comfortable perch. She requires the full power of her concentration to avoid sharp rocks, those fat, yellow scorpions, and the plethora of serpents that abound here. Do I aid her in this critical task? No, I squirm on her back like a disgruntled child. If she snuck off in the night I would not blame her. I imagine her only hope is that I shall return her to civilization. I share her longing.

Another of Serra's missions — abandoned. The houses still have goods in them: beds of rotting straw, rough-hewn wooden furniture, pots and pans. In one house a crib stands empty, a hand-woven blanket turned aside, as if the mother took the baby in haste and left behind its cherished blanket. Where did everyone go? Was it the natives? Did these people flee for their lives? There is no evidence of slaughter but the imagination supplies gruesome imagery nonetheless.

We camped, and I heard an unsettling howl from the mission. I cannot quite place it; although, it reminds me of a calf being slaughtered — a horrible lowing that speaks of a betrayal of trust. It keeps me awake. At first light, after my prayers, I inspect the mission. The sound? Wind blowing through the open windows, nothing more.

San Francisco: a hamlet tucked among rolling hills, a wide bay dwarfing it. More homes here. The mission is larger, in better shape. The others in our little party perk up at the sight of houses, roads, the promise of warmth, good food, and ample drink. Even my long-suffering pony quickens her step. Has her faith in me been restored?

There is activity at the mission, locals and natives. It is no market square, but a place of worship, for I can tell they venerate it. Yet when I ask to see the priest they act as if they do not understand or as if my question was frivolous. Finally, after much pestering on my part, one of the old women repeats, "He will come. He will come."

He will come? What does that mean?

I tried to organize a baptism. I tried to speak for the dead. I offered to hear confessions. They refused, politely at first, as if I should not labor on their behalf, with less patience later, as if I were offending. When I demanded to see the priest they took me to a room in the mission and closed the door behind me. When I opened it I saw that a pair of natives stood guard. They smiled but when I tried to leave the room they barred the way and shook their heads, still smiling.

He will come? I begin to fear it.

Brother Gonçalo lay in the narrow bed, watching the candlelight flicker on the dull brown wood of the door, the other side of which stood two native guards. He rolled over onto his side against the wall, closed his eyes, and tried to be thankful for the bed. It was something. When he heard the door open he lifted his head and look over his shoulder.

The two guards peered in. They held torches, the resin popping. They stared at Gonçalo for some time, he staring back. They parted and a third man stepped into the doorway. The torchlight behind him was stronger than the candle in front, throwing his face into shadow. Gonçalo turned onto his back and reached for the candle. Quick movement from the man paused his arm.

Gonçalo tried to sit up but the man stepped to him and placed a hand on his chest, preventing him. The man was within the candle's light now and Gonçalo could see him. He was old, tremendously old, but only from the neck up. Gonçalo could feel the strength in his body, for the pressure of his hand was like a full grown bull lying atop him. When the man was certain Gonçalo would not rise he removed his hand. The two guards shut the door. The room fell into semi-darkness. The old man pulled a chair from the corner and sat, facing Gonçalo.

"Are you the—"

"It is a shame you have come here, Brother," said the man. His voice was eloquent, it displayed learning. "Am I the parish priest?" asked the man. He smiled. "I am Junípero Serra."

"But you—you can't be." The old man remained silent. "He would be—"

"I am one hundred and nineteen years old," said Serra.

"But that's—impossible."

"How old was Methuselah? How old was Abraham when he died?" Serra turned and looked at the candle. The craggy terrain of his face was defined by its flickering light. He frowned. "Your arrival here threatens all I have built." He glanced at Gonçalo but returned his eyes to the candle's flame.

"I haven't come to—"

Serra turned his dark eyes to Gonçalo. "Why have you come?"

"The Archbishop said that your missions—" But the stern gaze of the old man killed the words in Gonçalo.

Serra chuckled. "I had forgotten all about Archbishops, Popes, Rome, Madrid—all of it." He looked now kindly at Gonçalo. He extended his hand and Gonçalo got the impression he wanted his hand so he pulled it from under the blanket. The old man took it and studied it. "No callouses." He released Gonçalo's hand. "Are you a scribe? Do you copy ancient tomes? Do you roam the library stacks searching for—for what?"

"I—"

"I too was searching," said Serra, "although I did not know it. I thought I had found it, my peace, my certainty. I was mistaken. I came up here all those years ago." He waved a hand. "There was nothing. Some deer. A brown bear. Eden—before Adam and Eve." He rubbed his hands together, staring at the candle's flame.

"I tried to convert the natives. I only succeeded in amusing them with my piety, my earnestness. They demanded miracles. I demanded faith." He smiled. "They said they would show me miracles." He rose, plucked the chair from the floor, and set it in the corner.

"Do you remember," he began, his back to Gonçalo. "When Moses and his people were lost in the desert?" He turned, sunk in gloom, the candle's light barely reaching him. "They begged Moses to do something, anything, to end their misery. He had no answers." Serra stepped forward. "What did the people do? They sought out something, anything to aid them. What did they find?"

"A false idol."

"A bull," said Serra. "To be specific. They made an idol of a bull and offered it sacrifices. What happened then?"

"God got angry."

"Why?"

"His people had no faith," said Gonçalo.

"No, that isn't why," said Serra. "He got angry because he was afraid." Gonçalo gasped but Serra continued. "His chosen people had suffered much. They had asked—begged—that he do something. When he did nothing they sought out strength. The wilderness does that —makes people seek strength. When I arrived here—" Serra frowned. "No, not yet. What did God do next?"

"He called Moses to the mountaintop."

"Yes, and gave him laws for his people to follow. This he did," Serra pointed to the ceiling, "because he was afraid."

"You blasphemy!"

Serra smiled. "Forgive me. I do not mean to offend you—your beliefs."

"*My* beliefs? Not yours?"

Serra turned and looked at the candle's flame. "I've built something here. Something strong. That's what is needed—in the wilderness." He looked at Gonçalo. "Strength." He smiled. "The natives showed me how. Their ways are simple, primitive, even, but strong."

"Pagans!"

Serra studied Gonçalo's face. "Pagan? I had forgotten that ugly word. No, this won't do. I cannot explain—it cannot be explained." He stepped to Gonçalo and reached out, gripping his shoulder. With inhuman strength he lifted Gonçalo from the bed and set him on his feet. "I must show you, it is the only way. Get dressed."

Junípero Serra led Gonçalo through the dark halls of the mission. The two native guards followed, the light from their torches leaping along the ceiling and walls. Gonçalo heard whispering ahead. The quintet emptied into the main chapel. It was half full of natives. They sat on the floor, their legs crossed, passing a long pipe between them. The aromatic odor of the smoke filled the chapel. When Serra entered they stood.

"The altar," said Serra, motioning. Gonçalo looked. It was not a Christian alter. It was a low, wide table made of iron, stained dark, and perforated. Serra motioned and Gonçalo stepped up and looked down. "What do you make of it?"

Gonçalo looked at the old man beside him. There was more light on him now and Gonçalo could see the pronounced musculature beneath his robe. His shoulders bulged. His chest was broad and deep. His hands were wide. Only his neck and face showed the one hundred and nineteen years he claimed.

"I—" Gonçalo looked away from Serra. "I don't know."

Serra came around him and stood looking down at the iron table. "There is an ancient ritual, begun in Persia," he looked at Gonçalo. "Taurobolium. Have you heard if it?"

Gonçalo heard shuffling movement and looked. The chapel was filling with locals and natives. Where, Gonçalo wondered, had they come from and at this hour. They packed together, squeezing into the room. They said naught. Other than the shuffling and their breathing there was only the voice of Serra.

Serra continued. "The neophyte was placed here," he knelt and motioned beneath the iron table. "He lay on his back." Serra reached out and gripped the edge of the table. "A bull was led here, to stand atop."

As Serra spoke there was a commotion at the edge of the room. The people began to jostle against one another and pack tighter together. Gonçalo looked and tried to see what was happening but there were too many people.

Serra stood. "Make room," he commanded. The people parted. Gonçalo saw that one of the two guards who had stood outside of his door, and that had escorted him here, now led a bull into the chapel. In one hand he held the resin torch, in the other the bull's knotted lead. The second guard followed.

"The bull's throat is cut," said Serra, speaking now at Gonçalo's ear. Gonçalo turned but he could not move back, for the people pressed. "The blood spills down onto the table's top. It runs through the holes, onto he who waits below." Serra nodded and Gonçalo felt many hands grab him.

"What? No!"

"The neophyte rubs the blood into his skin; his chest, his neck, his face." Serra nodded and the hands tore the robe from Gonçalo.

"What are you doing?"

"I'm showing you, Brother. I'm showing you what the people of Moses knew. What the pagans knew. What the natives here *know*. I'm showing you—strength." Again Serra nodded and Gonçalo, despite his protestations, was made to lie beneath the perforated iron table.

Serra knelt. Gonçalo could hear the bull being led onto the table. He could hear the clack-clack of its hooves against the iron. Someone spoke and Serra looked up. He reached and when his hand came again into view it held a long, slender knife.

"In the Pentateuch," said Serra, "there is a prohibition against the drinking of blood." He began to quote the lines from memory. "For *it is* the life of all flesh, the blood *is* the life thereof; therefore I said unto the children of Israel, Ye shall not eat of the blood of any manner of flesh, for the life of all *is* the blood thereof; whosoever eateth it shall be cut off."

Gonçalo fought against the hands that held him. He was not strong enough to break their hold. He turned and looked at Serra, his gaze full of fear. "I beg you, do not do this!"

"Your god is weak, Brother. Your god is afraid. My god," he glanced at the bull, then returned his eyes to Gonçalo, "is powerful."

"No!" Screamed Gonçalo.

"You shall eateth of the blood, Brother. It will sink into your flesh and you will know," he pointed the knife at Gonçalo. "You will know that your god was right—the blood *is* the life." Serra stood.

"No!" Screamed Gonçalo.

He heard the bull's hooves rattle on the iron. He heard the gurgling cut. He heard the bull's lifeblood splash against the iron table above him. He tried to squirm, to turn away, but was held fast. The blood began to drip from the holes. The bull tried to low, to condemn, but its throat had been slashed. It slumped onto its belly. The blood poured now from the holes, a hundred rivulets, coating Gonçalo's nude body. Hands reached beneath the table and began to rub the blood into his flesh. The blood splashed against his face.

"No!"

"Yes, Brother!" yelled Serra from above, unseen. "The blood will wash away your false beliefs!"

"No!" And with that final scream, Gonçalo ate of the blood.

WIFE, WOLF, AND WOODSMAN

Smith, Jedediah Strong, 1790-1831, American explorer, one of the greatest of the Mountain Men, b. not far from Binghamton, N.Y. He seems to have arrived in St. Louis in 1822 and to have joined the expedition of William H. Ashley, but little is known of his part on that first expedition. On the 1823 expedition he was prominent.

A young man more than 6ft. tall and devoted to Bible reading, he was a superb rifleman and dauntless in trouble. When the expedition was stopped by an attack of the Arikara Indians, he headed a party sent to ask help. After returning he went down to St. Louis and back up the river to join the expedition.

Early in 1824 he and Thomas Fitzpatrick took a party through South Pass and thus started regular use of that route, which had been used by Robert Stuart and his party from Astoria in 1812. Smith and a few men went north, aided (and took the furs from) a group of Iroquois in the employ of the Hudson's Bay Company and with Alexander Ross went to the country of the Flathead Indians in present Montana. He went as far north as the present Canadian boundary, then came back to the Great Salt Lake.

In 1825 he set out on his most famous venture. From the Great Salt Lake he set out to the southwest and with a small band of men pushed across the Colorado River and the Mojave Desert to arrive in San Diego, Calif.; the Spanish of the western settlements were startled and not too please to see them. They were relieved when Smith and two of his men went east, the first white men, as far as is known, to cross the Sierra Nevada and the fearsome

Great Salt Desert. They arrived at the rendezvous in the summer of 1827. Smith and a party went again on the southwestern route to California. They were set upon by the Mohave Indians, but the survivors reached California and the men who had been left there. After some trouble with the Mexican authorities, Smith and his men went north....

- The Columbia Encyclopedia

Jedediah sat on a felled log at the edge of the light, back warmed by the fire, front chilled by the wooded depths. The camp was quiet. Only the crackle of the fire sounded. The light flickered among the branches above, coloring and warming tree-flesh. The shadows surrounding the camp were alive, agitated by firelight.

The subdued sounds of the nighttime forest enveloped them in gentle company: the low-throated hooting of owls, the clipped chatter of foxes, the cautious sniffing of an opossum. In the distance a predator moved ponderously, unafraid of the threat of night.

The men were reclining, occupied with thought and rumination, their pipes assisting. Jedediah moved his right hand from his lap and reached behind him without turning, groping for his rifle. His fingers fell on its hickory stock. He dragged it from its leather holster—a dull scrape that threatened—and slid it onto his thighs.

One of his men, Thomas Longmate, caught the movement and knew enough not to stir or call out. He ceased puffing his pipe and turned his eyes—without turning his head—the direction Jedediah was looking. He reached—inch-by-inch—towards his own rifle. After many run-ins with natives, they were quick to arms.

What Jedediah saw, that Thomas did not, was a pair of dark, glossy eyes watching from the edge of the ragged circle of light. The eyes, on account of the firelight, flickered with orange, yellow, and red. Jedediah knew it was no human gaze, but it held a human intelligence.

He had seen plenty in his travels that he could not explain—and refused to try. The Bible—which Jedediah knew to be an infallible guide—spoke of devils and evil spirits. Jedediah need not call upon his imagination to know them. He stared into devil eyes now.

"Jed? What is it?" whispered Thomas. The men, being thus roused, turned their attention to their leader. Getting no response they turned to Thomas, who nodded. The men grabbed their rifles and stood. Thomas stood too and went to Jedediah, crouching. He gazed into the darkness. He brought his rifle up but wasn't sure where to aim. Jedediah turned as a rifle's barrel entered his peripheral vision. "What d'ya see?" whispered Thomas. Jedediah looked back to the darkness but the eyes were gone.

"Nothing."

"But—yer rifle."

"Get some sleep."

Thomas withdrew.

"Thomas." Jedediah glanced over his shoulder, then returned his gaze to the darkness. "Say your prayers."

. . .

Juan was weak with hunger and had to sit. A ledge of exposed rock made for a welcome seat, its mossy covering an aid to comfort. He had lost the doe. Was she too much to hope for? he wondered. His was the thinking of a penitent; that God would not allow such bounty, not while they were in a state of sin.

His father's rifle was heavy in his hands. A hare, which had been standing stock still, shot off, dodging beneath a broad, low-hung leaf. He meant to raise the rifle, but his arms were stuck as though in tar. He thought of his father and wondered how much longer he would survive. He rose and began again, hoping to pick up the doe's tracks.

He rounded a spruce and lowered a branch from the neighboring tree. In the space behind it was a man. His face showed no discernible emotion. Juan took a reflexive step back and the branch leapt from his hand.

He heard movement behind him and saw another man. He turned, as yet another stranger came into view. Both men were holding rifles, not aimed at him, but menacing still.

The branch moved and the first man sighted ducked beneath. He was a foot taller than Juan. He stepped up, reached out, and took the rifle from Juan's hands—gently —as if lifting it from its perch above the mantle. He examined it. More men stepped into the open, all white skinned but one, a Negro.

Juan studied the apparition before him. The man was tall and lean. His shoulders were wide but the hunger-thinness to his chest made his leather jerkin hang flat. He wore deer-skin breeches and beaver-skin boots. Beneath the jerkin was a loose cotton shirt. A knife the length and width of a man's forearm hung from his belt in a tasseled sheath. Its handle was deer antler. A rifle was slung across his back. He wore an assortment of feathered, bone-beaded charms about his person. Gifts, no doubt, from the peoples he had encountered. Gifts, thought Juan, or souvenirs of battle.

The white man's pale blond hair was medium in length and somewhat unkempt. It swept across his forehead. His eyes were large and of a striking brightness. He must have recently shaved, perhaps using the knife at his hip. His face had been roughened by the blade but was clean of hair.

He was a man—one could tell—who deliberated with great effort but who acted swiftly and with resolution. He was a type of man, in more ways than one, that Juan had never encountered before. There was something about the tall white man that Juan could not identify. He did not know, and would be unable to comprehend if he did, that the man before him had begun civilized but had become, over the course of his travels in the wild middle of the new continent, *un*civilized.

The tall man tucked Juan's rifle under one arm. He reached out with his other hand and ran his fingers down the lapel of Juan's coat. He pulled it open and looked beneath. Juan did not understand why, at first, but he surmised that the man was searching for a pistol. He said something in a language Juan did not know but that he believed was English. One of the other white men stepped up and took the rifle.

The tall white man spoke to Juan. All he understood was his name, "Jedediah." Juan shook his head. The man spoke in yet another language. Juan knew it to be native, but he did not know it. Again the man switched tongues. Again Juan shook his head. The man turned and looked at the Negro, who stepped up.

"Who are you?" asked the Negro in broken Spanish, speaking with an accent that Juan could not place.

"My name," Juan looked between the Negro and the tall white man whose unblinking gaze bored into him, "is Juan Bautista Alvarado."

"What are you doing out here?" asked the Negro.

"Hunting."

The Negro told this to Jedediah, who thought, then spoke. The man holding Juan's rifle returned it him.

"You're loud," said the Negro. "And the wind has betrayed you."

"My father—" Began Juan but the emotion of the situation threatened to overcome him. He turned, found the shelf of rock again, set his father's rifle against his knees, and dropped his head into his hands. He did not see Jedediah motion towards him. A tap on his shoulder alerted him. He raised his head. The Negro held out a bladder.

"Drink."

Juan lifted the spout to his lips and took sip. The whiskey burned his mouth and throat. He coughed. The Negro dug in a satchel and pulled out a folded piece of checkered cloth. He looked to Jedediah, who nodded, then held out the packet to Juan. The bladder of whiskey was exchanged for the folded cloth.

"What is—"

"Eat," said the Negro. "Sam Brock. Carolina way." He winked. "Escaped." Juan took the packet and unfolded it. He dug in the cloth and produced a hunk of dried fish. "You look a sight." Sam laughed. "Like I must have, two weeks free from that fat bastard's whip, half-starved, half-naked, and half-chewed by the hounds that came after." He winked again. "Bashed their skulls to teach 'em." Sam took a swig of whiskey and wiped his lips with the back of his hand. "Learned me some Spanish from a Jamaican, Kingston way, escaped too. Roomed with him in St. Louis before—" He paused, studying Juan's sunken cheeks.

Juan spoke between bites. "My father, he is sick. My mother tends to him, but his condition— We have not received a shipment of food in months. Hunting has been bad, fishing worse. God is angry with us. There is a mission not far but—" He shook his head. "We are—"

"Drink," said Sam, extending the bladder. Juan did so. "Your father?"

"He weakens."

Sam frowned and looked to Jedediah. He passed along the information. Jedediah spoke in return. Sam nodded and looked to Juan. "Where do you live?" Juan told him and Sam told Jedediah. Jedediah spoke. Sam turned back to Juan. "We will return you to your father." He looked at Jedediah, who was looking at Juan, his face inscrutable. "He will hunt for you."

. . .

Hunting in a strange wood at night is no easy task but Jedediah knew a trick. There are far better hunters than man yet they fear man. Jedediah sat quiet in a dark spot. He heard the squealing pain of violent death, rose, and began towards it. He smelled blood, heard sounds of movement, stopped, and waited—rifle in hand—half-sunk in the branches of a spruce.

He was surprised to see, illuminated by moonlight, a single black-furred wolf dragging a kid by the neck. The goat was dead so it offered no resistance other than its weight, which, Jedediah surmised, couldn't be great, young as it was. Still, the wolf struggled with its kill.

Jedediah was puzzled. Why and to where was the wolf dragging the goat? If it was hungry or feared for its prize why didn't it eat? If it had pups where were they? He watched the wolf approach and saw that it was emaciated, its ribs showing. Its legs were long and lean, its hips pronounced.

It must be, he guessed, weak from hunger or illness. That's why it struggled and that's why, he thought, it behaved against type. The wolf dropped the kid, ears perked, and listened. It sniffed, then turned to where Jedediah stood. Those eyes, thought Jedediah, those devil eyes. He'd seen them before.

He raised his rifle, aimed at the wolf that stood not three yards from him, and pulled the trigger. The wolf was quicker and dropped flat onto its stomach. The shot went over. It rose, charged, and leapt, striking Jedediah in the chest, biting at his face, his rifle knocked from his hands. The pair fell out of the spruce and rolled. Jedediah tossed the wolf aside, rose into a crouch, and drew his knife.

The wolf got to its feet, turned towards Jedediah, its fur rising, and growled. Blood dripped from its fangs and slicked the fur of its breast. Its eyes were yellowed with hunger and rage.

"Ain't no wolf come at a man like that," whispered Jedediah. "What manner of beast are you?"

The wolf shot forward and snapped but Jedediah swung the knife in a fast arc and the wolf darted back, still growling.

"Give me the kid," said Jedediah. "Go fetch you another."

The wolf feinted to Jedediah's left, away from the knife, but when Jedediah turned the wolf shifted to his right and bit, but only caught the loose sleeve of his shirt between its teeth. Jedediah grabbed the wolf's scruff with his left hand and rose, plucking the wolf from the earth. The wolf released his shirt, twisted its head, and tried to bite the hand that held it.

Jedediah thrust the knife, aiming for the wolf's heart, but the beast squirmed. The wrenching motion broke Jedediah's grip and threw him off balance. The wolf yelped in pain, for the knife had got it still. It landed awkwardly, flopping, and came up on three legs, holding its left leg aloft.

Jedediah stumbled in reverse, caught himself, and crouched, holding the bloodied blade before him. The wolf eyed him, growling. It backed away, turned, and ran as well as it could on three legs, the kid abandoned. Jedediah watched the wolf until it disappeared. He wiped his knife on his breeches and sheathed it, then bent to scoop up the kid. He paused, for the wolf's severed paw lay quivering in a pool of blood.

"Hand of the Devil," mused Jedediah. He plucked the paw from the pool and stuffed it into a leather bag on his belt, replacing the compass, which he pulled free. He scooped up the kid and threw it over his shoulder. He found a beam of moonlight and thrust the compass within.

. . .

"Father?" Juan sat in a chair beside his father's sick bed. "There are men."

The old man's eyes fluttered and he turned his head to face his son. He motioned, his hand lifting mere inches from the quilt, for his strength was naught. Juan took a cloth from a water-filled porcelain bowl and dabbed the sweat from his father's fevered brow. He tried not to look, but saw anyway, the blood-stained strip of cotton wrapped around his father's throat. It hid a wound that would not heal, no matter what was done.

"Son?"

"Yes?"

"Your mother?"

Juan shook his head. "To hunt, maybe, or to fetch—"

"Men?"

"White men, Father."

His father's eyes widened and he lifted his head. "Here?" Juan nodded. "No, son." The old man returned his head to the pillow. "You have the sickness, like me. I've seen—"

"No, Father." Juan returned the washcloth to the bowl. "They make a camp outside. They say," he chuckled, "they will suffer no roof over their heads. They are strange men, Father."

"Mexican," the old man said, "the moonlight—"

"Father, please, listen. They're white men, from the east. Why they've come, I cannot say, but they've come."

His father looked hard at him. "Their leader?"

"He comes," Juan smiled, "with food."

"When your mother returns," said his father, "send her to me."

. . .

Jedediah paused. At the top of the hill was a house, shingled in rough wood, but otherwise the most civilized thing he had seen in months. Light shone from its windows. Wisps of silver smoke curled from its stone chimney. He saw, also, the light of a camp fire at the bottom the hill.

He glanced up at the moon then looked down at the gravel path that led up to the house. It was as he thought, the trail of blood led here. He had caught glimpses of the blood in the woods when the moonlight fell upon it. He knelt and dipped his fingertips into the livid streak— warm. He stood, wiped the blood on his breeches, and walked to the camp.

"Whatcha got there?" asked Sam.

"Kid."

"I'll go up with ya." Sam rose, knocked his pipe stem against his palm to empty the bowl, and fell in along side Jedediah. "Ain't been in a proper home in," he laughed, "recent memory."

When the pair were halfway up the hill, and out of earshot of the camp, Jedediah slowed his pace. "Sam."

"Eh?"

"Wolf come this way?"

"Huh?"

"Wolf on three legs, a bloody stump for the fourth?"

"Ain't *never* seen me a wolf like that."

Jedediah motioned with a nod of his head. Sam looked down then knelt. "Fresh," he said, looking up at Jedediah. "You think—" He scanned the gravel path.

"Veers off." He pointed. "Gone around back." He stood. "Ain't no wounded wolf gonna go near a man's home. Hell, a wounded wolf, *any* wounded animal, is gonna do damn near the opposite." He glanced at Jedediah. "Gonna find himself a hole to hide in."

"Herself."

"Huh?"

"Female."

Sam looked from Jedediah to the house. "Could be they got one trained."

"Could be."

. . .

Jedediah stopped at the door and held out the kid. Sam took it but studied the other man's face. "Ain'tcha goin' in?" Only a slight turn of the head gave the answer. "You goin' 'round back?" A slight nod answered. "Boss, you take them men with ya, now, ya hear?"

"What's begun," said Jedediah, "was begun betwixt me and her. It's gotta be finished as such." Sam gazed upon Jedediah's face a moment longer, nodded, then opened the door and entered.

. . .

"My wife," said Juan's father, upon hearing boots enter. "Should have greeted—" He stopped when he beheld a brown-skinned face, for he was expecting white.

"Father," said Juan, "this man is Sam Brock."

"A pleasure," said Sam.

"He's brought a goat. Soon we'll have—"

"From whence have you come, Sam Brock?"

"Carolina way."

"Carolina?"

"East, along that great big ocean."

"You come with white men?" asked Juan's father. Sam nodded. "Do you lead—"

"Ain't none of us really lead, to put it that way." Sam rubbed his chin. "But Jedediah," he smiled, "well, we trust 'em. He fetched that billygoat for ya, out of them dark woods yonder." He studied the ill man. "Hey, now, how you come about that?" He motioned to the blood-blotted cotton wrap.

. . .

Jedediah followed the trail of blood to the outhouse door. It was closed. A streak of blood, so dark as to look black, ran in a jagged line, guided by the valleys in the vertical boards. He stood, clear in the moonlight, and listened. Labored breathing—breathing, not panting— came from within. He drew his knife, reached out, and opened the door.

She was sprawled on the bench, her glossy black hair matted against her forehead and cheeks. She was nude, the sheen of sweat on her ochre skin reflected the moonlight, made deeper the shadow. She clutched her left wrist with her right hand. The blood had coagulated and made an ugly cap on the stump of her arm. She rolled her eyes to Jedediah and spoke with a halting voice, but what she said he didn't know. She was lean of limb, her torso flat, her hip bones made prominent by hunger. A tuft of sweat-glistened pubic hair showed, half in shadow, half in light.

He sheathed his knife. He reached out and pulled the hair from her eyes. She looked at him and he at her. He felt for the pouch, untied it by feel, then plunged his hand in, feeling for the paw. He felt not fur but human flesh. He pulled the hand free and held it, not yet looking, but staring into the woman's dark eyes.

He looked down and verified with his eyes what his touch knew. He held no wolf's severed paw, but a woman's hand. He returned the hand to his pouch, cinched it tight but didn't tie it, then reached out and shut the door.

. . .

Juan, his father, and their visitor heard the door below open and shut. They heard boots on the wooden stairs. All three waited in silence. Sam moved a hand to his knife.

Jedediah appeared in the doorway. He stood and surveyed the room. He ducked and entered, coming to the sick man's bedside. He spoke. Sam, taken aback, did not translate. When his wits returned, he spoke, although he kept his gaze on Jedediah.

"He wants to know, where is your wife?"

"My wife?"

Juan spoke, "Have you not seen her? Is she not downstairs?"

Jedediah turned his gaze to Juan, held it there for a moment, then turned back to the sick man. He spoke. Sam translated.

"He says, when he was in the wood, he came across a black-haired wolf. She killed the kid and he meant to take it from her. They fought and he severed her forepaw. Boss?" asked Sam, in English, for Jedediah reached into a bag at his belt, but paused, his hand hidden within. Again he spoke and again Sam translated. "He says, after the fight, he took her paw." Sam looked at the sick man. "He wants to show it to you."

"But why?" began Juan. "What foolishness is this? What—"

Jedediah drew his hand from the leather bag. The three men turned their eyes. They expected to see a wolf's black-furred paw but instead they saw a human hand; spotted with blood, mud under the nails, slender-fingered, and small in Jedediah's hand. Juan gasped. The old man looked away. Only Sam spoke. "Where did ya get that hand?"

Jedediah spoke but not in answer. Sam turned to Juan. "He wants to know if you recognize it." At this, Jedediah held out the hand. Juan bent and looked. He looked up at Jedediah, to the hand, then to his father.

"Father!"

The old man stared at the ceiling. It was some time before he spoke. "Since I fell ill," he began, "since the fever came, I dream. Every night at the darkest hour, when the light of Christ is furthest and the Devil close, I dream that I am awaken by a black she-wolf." He turned his head and looked at the hand Jedediah held in his own. He returned his gaze to the ceiling above. "She slinks quietly into my marriage bed. She lays beside me and licks this wound." He lifted his hand, to point to the wound in his neck, but succeeded only in pointing feebly to the far wall. "In this dream she laps my blood." He breathed, a raspy sound. "A fever-dream." Tears formed, broke, and ran down his sunken cheeks into the black-and-silver hair of his short beard. When he spoke his voice was thick. "My own wife —a monster!"

"Father! What are you—" Juan looked from his father to Sam to Jedediah. "My mother—" He forced himself to look at the hand. He looked back up at Jedediah. Emotion overtook him. He reached out with both hands and grabbed the leather jerkin. "What have you done!"

Sam grabbed Juan's wrists. "Careful, now." But he need not worry. Jedediah made no movement.

"Son!" The sick man reached out and placed his hand on his son's wrist. "Bring no violence to my house. Have we not enough?"

Juan released Jedediah, fell seated on the edge of his father's bed, and covered his face with his hands. "Father! It cannot be true!" He lifted his head. "These men—no! They are *not* men!" He stood, shoulders thrust forward, left hand balled into a fist, right pointing to Jedediah's chest. Spittle flew, his features wild with emotion. "Phantoms! Evil spirits—sent by the Devil himself! The Devil's hand—"

"Boy—" began Sam, but movement from Jedediah stopped him. Jedediah bent and placed the severed hand on the table next to the porcelain bowl. He turned and began out of the room but stopped in the doorway, speaking over his shoulder.

"He says," began Sam, "your wife is in the outhouse. He says, it ain't his place to kill a man's wife, being a Christian, but that he *will* kill her," Sam looked at Juan then at his father, "if you ask him to."

"I have no wife."

"Father!" Juan knelt and took his father's hand into his. Tears wet both faces. He spoke low, urgent but cautious, feeling the enemy was too near to avoid. "Heed not the word of—"

"Son," said the sick man. He reached with his other hand and set it on the back of Juan's. He looked into his son's eyes. "Can a man be wed to a beast?"

"But, Father, these men cannot be trusted. Would we believe what they say? White men? From," he glanced up at Sam, "Carolina?" He leaned close to his father and spoke in a whisper. "They have taken— They have cut—" He glanced sidelong at Jedediah. "They conspire to rob you of your wife and me of my mother." He stood but still gripped his father's hands. "I beg you— No! I demand—"

"My wound, Son. Forget not my wound. Did I not dream of a black she-wolf long before these men came? Did they know this? Did *you*? And yet," he glanced at Sam, then returned his gaze to his son, "they beheld a black wolf."

Jedediah ducked once more and left the room. The three men listened to his boots on the wooden steps.

. . .

The outhouse door was closed but he knew she wasn't within. He could feel her absence. Still, he drew his knife and opened the door. He turned and scanned the moonlit tree line. He listened. He sniffed the air for the hint of blood. He knelt and scanned the grass for the sight of it. He stood and sheathed his knife.

She was gone.

PROPHECY

A warning to the reader: This story is based on an ancient Greek myth. It contains descriptions of suffering and violence that will be upsetting to most.

Excerpted from **California**. After having briefly asserted the independence of California in 1836, the Californios drove out (1845) the last Mexican governor. Under the influence of John C. Frémont the Americans set up (1846) a republic at Sonoma under the Bear Flag. The news of war between the United States and Mexico reach California soon afterward. On July 7, 1846, Commodore John D. Sloat captured Monterey, the capital, and claimed California for the United States; in 1847 Stephen W. Kearny defeated the Californios in the south. By the treaty of Guadalupe Hidalgo (1848) Mexico formally ceded the territory to the United States. In the same year occurred the most significant event in California history—while establishing a sawmill for Sutter near Coloma, James W. Marshall discovered gold and touched off the California gold rush.

- The Columbia Encyclopedia

Hernando Cruz y Navarro, the last Mexican governor of California, had been dumped into a shallow grave. Before this, he had been beaten with iron rods and burned with torches until his face was black and his lips burned away to the gums. He was not dead when he was buried but was expected to die.

When Hernando was taken from his office by a mob of Californios, his secretary—who was just then returning and saw the mob drag Hernando into the street—ran to the governor's home. There, he told Hernando's young wife what had happened.

She was, at that moment, breastfeeding the couple's infant son. Hernando's wife, Maria, was so shocked she could not act. The secretary, fearing for her and the infant, gathered the pair and hurried them from the house, leaving all things of comfort behind.

The secretary led them into the wilderness at the edge of town. He returned with the hope of either placating the mob, saving Hernando, or, failing these, misdirecting them from mother and child. When Hernando's secretary saw that his employer was being beaten and burned, his courage left him and he fled.

. . .

The sun was sullen-red just above the cool-blue ocean, making shadows long and wavy-edged. Hernando, the taste of charcoal and earth on his tongue, tried to open his eyes and found he could not. The orbital bone under his right eye had been shattered by an iron pipe—his eye swollen shut. The lid of his other eye was pressed shut by the weight of the soil atop it.

He did not know that he was buried and left for dead. He tried to lift his arm and remove the weight from his eye but found there was weight atop all of him. His mind did not long contemplate his situation. His mind, after his treatment at the hands of the Californios, was—like the bones of his face—shattered.

. . .

A man reached into the fox's den and grabbed Maria by the hair. He yanked her out.

"Please!" screamed Maria. "Mercy, please, I beg you!"

"Full-throated one. Ha! You have led me to your mother! Could you not cover his mouth? Eh? Or were you too frightened to think of it?"

"Have you found her, Diego?"

"Yes. See?"

A second man came and held the torch aloft. "Yes, it is she, the Governor's wife. The baby, too, is his."

"Please, in the name of God—" cried Maria. One of the men kicked her. She toppled over and the infant nearly rolled from her arms, but did not.

"We have removed your husband from office," said the man with the torch.

"We are a free people," said the other man. He turned and yelled to the others who had been searching. He turned back to Maria. "No more rule from afar. No more of *your* kind."

The rest of the men and women came up and looked at Maria and her infant son.

"What shall we do with her?"

"What do the people do in a revolution?"

Maria was yanked to her feet—clutching her infant son in her arms.

. . .

Hernando crouched and studied the buildings nearby. To his grave-eyes they were mere shapes of contrasting light and dark, made so by the setting sun. He did not recognize them. He looked down at the ruptured grave. It seemed more a home to him than the buildings of man. The wet, clinging grip of soil had been more intimate than the fleeting caress of the cool breeze from the ocean.

For a moment he thought to return to the earth but he heard loud shouts coming down the hill and was curious. He grabbed the earth-caked, bloodied, black robe that had been his shroud, tossed it over his shoulders, and went towards the voices.

. . .

The mob of Californios pushed, kicked, slapped, and otherwise harassed Maria from the wilderness to the town.

38

She stumbled and often fell, but always managed to turn and land on her shoulder, keeping the crying infant from being crushed. They singed her dress and hair with their torches, laughing all the while.

When they reached the town square they surrounded her. They whispered amongst themselves, their voices barely rising above the crackle of the torches. Maria tried to beg for her own life and the life of her infant son, but tears would not allow her speak. The men went off in search of something, Maria knew not what. A woman came to her.

"We've voted," said the woman. Other women stood around, looking at Maria and her infant. "We're going to burn you at the stake."

"My child—"

The woman looked at the tightly-clutched infant. She stepped up, reached out, and placed her hand on Maria's cheek. "Yes, your child too."

. . .

Hernando stood in the last fleeting shadows and watched. The sun set and the moon was revealed. The activity of the people was illuminated by the torches they held. He was confused by their activity and went closer.

. . .

The men returned with long branches, faggots, and dry reeds. They made a pile around a tall stake driven into the ground. A man came with an iron hoop. Maria watched, trapped by the women, unable to believe what was happening to her. When the pyre was built the men came and grabbed Maria.

"Please," she begged, "take him." She held out her infant. The women did not take him.

The men lifted her atop the pyre and positioned the iron hoop around her waist, to bind her to the stake. They stuffed a bladder of gunpowder between her breasts and the infant. At first Maria thought to lift her arms and let the bladder drop then she thought, perhaps, it would make the death of her son quicker. She squeezed her arms tighter.

"Maria Cruz y Navarro," announced one of the men, who was, before the revolution, a stevedore, lugging crates onto the dock, but who, now that the revolution was on, was a self-appointed executioner. "We are a free people. This land is ours. It does not belong to the rich nobles in Mexico City. *We* do not belong to them!" At this, the Californios cheered.

The man turned from Maria and her infant, who cried, and addressed the gathered crowd. "I ask you, how has it always been? Eh? Since the dawn of civilization, how has it always been? They," he pointed at Maria, "the nobles, the rich and powerful, rule. We labor and they take! We work and they," he turned to Maria and sneered, "they *do not* work." He stepped to a man who held a torch and took it from him but he was not yet done.

"We are the people. We are the many. It is upon *our* backs that all this is built." He waved his hand. "But they, like a parasite, drain the life from us." He spun and looked at the gathered mob. "We only have what *they* allow us to have!" He beat his chest with his fist. "Do I not work my fingers to the bone?" He pointed. "Do you?" He pointed. "Do you?" He turned to Maria. "Does she?" The crowd laughed. "No, she and her husband. They take! What do they do for us? Nothing! They take the fruits of our labors —our gold, our silver—and send it to Mexico City. What happens to our gold and silver in Mexico City? Go on, tell us."

"Please," moaned Maria between sobs. "My child— my infant son. He's innocent."

"For now!" Screamed the man. "What will he become? Eh? Another parasite!" He stepped to the edge of the pyre and leaned towards Maria. "We have suffered. Now it is time for you to suffer."

. . .

Hernando came to the edge of the circle of jostling bodies surrounding his wife and infant son. He listened. He tried to comprehend. The peace of the grave called to him. The insanity and violence of what he saw spoke louder. He screamed and the mob turned.

They did not recognize him. His face was black and broken, his eyes white and wild. His flesh, exposed through his ripped and bloodied shirt, was pale, his blood having seeped from his many wounds. He was inhuman, made so by their brutality. They recoiled away from the ghoul before them. He threw off his grave shroud.

"Beasts!" he screamed. The word was a shrill hiss, for his lips were no longer able to shape it. "Murderers!" He swept his arms out, his fingers now like claws, caked with blood and grave-dirt. "You condemn? You! Who have blood on your hands! My blood!"

He advanced. The mob parted. He arrived at the edge of the unlit pyre and climbed atop it. The stevedore-executioner threw the torch onto the pyre and it began to burn.

Maria screamed when she saw her husband. Hernando did not look at her. He grabbed the infant. The bladder of gunpowder fell. He turned and began down the pyre, stepping over the growing flames.

"The Devil possesses all of you!" screamed Hernando. "This is the land of the Devil! This is Hell!" As he spoke he ripped the thin fabric from his infant son.

"Husband!" cried Maria. "Help me!"

The flames leapt from the faggots to the reeds to the branches. The breeze fed the flames and blew the smoke free. The mob was stunned to inaction. They watched in horror as Hernando bit his infant son's thigh, his blackened teeth tearing the pale flesh. The infant screamed. He did not spit the flesh of his child out, but swallowed it without chewing.

"Is this how the Devil behaves?" asked Hernando. "Does he beat his victims? Does he burn them?" Hernando bit the stomach of his infant son and tore free a chunk, swallowing it. "Does he consume his victims like a wild beast? Tell me!"

The mob of Californios stood wide-eyed. The fire was roaring now and made a silhouette of Hernando.

Maria sobbed and wailed. The bladder of gunpowder exploded but did little to aid her. She looked up and begged, "Have mercy on me Jesus!" This was the last thing she was heard to say.

She beat upon her breast with her right arm, her left gripping the iron hoop. The fire consumed her clothing, leaving her nude. The fire turned black her flesh. While Maria burned, Hernando consumed his infant son. Soon the baby ceased crying. Still Maria screamed. Still Hernando screamed.

The fire burned Maria's legs, rendering the fat she had retained from the pregnancy. It pooled beneath her, bubbling. She beat her chest until her arm broke off and fell into the fire. She gripped the iron hoop, blood, water, and fat dripping from her fingertips. Her lower half consumed, her intestines and organs spilled from her and began to cook in the fire. She broke in half and fell forward, crashing into the branches. She could not be seen, nor heard.

"Devils!" screamed Hernando. "Hear your fate! Hear what God has in store for you!" He had consumed all but the head of his infant son. This he held aloft.

The mob looked. The infant's eyes opened. He blinked and frowned, looking first at one man, then another. "I sayeth unto you, those who have risen to the heights shall fall the farthest. I sayeth unto you," said the infant, "who have sinned against the natural order, that a reckoning cometh. Even now a reckoning cometh! You, who call yourself the Californios, shall be slain by Kearny, who wieldeth the sword of vengeance!" The infant fell silent and closed his eyes.

"So sayeth the Lord," growled Hernando. He stepped in reverse, into the fire, and was consumed.

THE RAKSHASA

Cochrane fled to the street. He was flustered and out of breath. He'd half-fallen down the stairs of his father's apartment, twisting his left ankle.

He'd burst from the door onto the street, only catching it at the last second to keep it from slamming against the wall. His clothes were disheveled, as was his hair. The shrouding darkness of the night stilled the swirl of emotions engulfing him. He breathed and tasted salt from the bay. He hid the blood on his shirt and jacket with his scarf and coat, ran a hand through his hair, remembered, looked, saw it was somehow, miraculously, clean, and slowed his pace to match those around him.

A nearby theater let out, filling the street with people. A cool breeze came from the Pacific, rushed up the winding, cobblestone avenues of San Francisco, blew away the horse-stench of the cabs then, upon reaching the top of the city, dissipated into the onyx sky. Cafés kept their street tables out. Seats began to fill, wine was consumed. The buildings on either side of the avenue reflected laughter and loud voices. A cabman, seeing Cochrane standing on the curb, snapped his whip and directed his horse.

"Where to, Sir?"

Cochrane, startled at being addressed, turned away. He slid along the wall, stepped into an alley, and placed his back to the still-warm brick. He tried to calm his racing mind.

What have I done?

The night sky, bright with diamond-hard stars and a close, crystalline moon, naked without clouds, now felt *too* open. The alley failed to confine his anxiety. A door opened to his left. He heard men crowding together. He went to the door, caught it as it was closing and stepped in.

The room was small, high-ceilinged, and luxuriously populated. Men stood in coattails, with polished, black leather shoes, and black bow-ties. They held their champagne flutes tight against their chests.

Their wives sat on ornate couches, wearing satins, silks, and uncomfortable shoes. They adorned their hair with flowers or wore fancy hats. Their throats were adorned with pearls or coral set in gold. The swooshing of Oriental fans moved what air managed to squeeze in the crowded room from outside before the door had been shut.

A stage had been pushed into a corner. It was little bigger than a milk crate. A man stood on it. He was neither young nor old. His skin was swarthy, giving his eyes a heightened whiteness. He was bearded to the edge of his lips and high up his cheeks. He wore a black suit, white shirt, and a black tie. He wore a red satin turban with a large emerald at the front. From behind the jewel rose an orange and yellow feather. At his waist was a short, curved dagger in an ornate silver sheath. The pommel was ebony wood studded with rubies. He looked over the crowd with inscrutable eyes.

Cochrane moved through the room, drawn by some unknown force closer to the foreigner. The crowd quieted.

"The beliefs of a culture," began the Indian, "define the possibilities it will allow." He spoke with a heavy accent but was intelligible. "That is, in this age of reason, people will be suspicious of any non-logical displays. Magic is no longer married to, and sanctified by, religion. Reason has exposed it as a trick, a subterfuge. Were I to throw a rope into the air, it fastening on the unseen, climb it, and disappear from sight, you would not be awed by magic, but search out some rational cause, a trap door, mirrors, some interference to your perception."

Many in the audience nodded. The Indian smiled, his white teeth shining in their dark frame. He looked over the audience, then continued.

"I admit that my culture, although ancient, is not as advanced as yours. Our religion governs our thinking. We've had our gods with us a long time. We are loath to be rid of them. We still think they bring us luck or ruin. The scientific outlook of the West has not yet penetrated far into the subcontinent of India. Were the people of some remote village to witness a man levitate, or have congress with cobras, or plunge a blade down his throat, they, unlike you, would grow worried, ask the gods to protect them and, as is often the case, give the magi whatever he desired so he would refrain from turning his powers on them."

This brought grumbles from the men, snickers from the women. The door opened. Cochrane looked. Someone exited. The door closed. When Cochrane looked back to the Indian the man's eyes were on him. The gaze was not without purpose, nor was it curious, but knowing, like a father who had witnessed a child misbehave.

In that moment the fear and paranoia that Cochrane felt, that had been subdued upon entering the room, flared. Cochrane believed he'd been found out. He feared that the blood showed. Or perhaps he was known to be an outsider, not belonging in the audience. When Cochrane was at the edge of panic, the Indian looked away.

"You would call such magi hucksters," said the Indian, "charlatans, preying upon the superstitions of simple people. You would be correct. However, as I said at the opening of this demonstration, certain things *are* permissible, if we all agree that they are. While clever men prey, intelligent men capitalize. In simple terms, magic *is* real." Despite the guffaws from the audience the Indian continued. "Magic is real because enough people believe it is real. Call it a form of energy, if you will, the energy of belief. Those schooled and practiced in such arts can manipulate this energy to great effect." The Indian shifted on his miniature stage. "You did not come to hear me speak, but to see me do. So be it. You, sir, come here." The room's eyes turned to Cochrane. "Come," commanded the Indian.

Without thinking, for he could not order his thoughts, or command his own actions, Cochrane advanced and stood at the foot of the stage.

"What is your name?" asked the Indian.

Cochrane had enough presence of mind to lie.

"Where have you come from?"

"A performance," said Cochrane, lying again.

"Did this performance involve a betrayal?" asked the Indian.

Cochrane was dumbfounded.

"Did this performance involve murder? Specifically, patricide?"

"No!" Cochrane shook his head. "No."

"Are you not a murderer?" asked the Indian.

Gasps of surprise from the audience. The Indian looked over Cochrane's head. "Witness, there is nothing in my hands." He shook his arms and held open his sleeves. "I conceal nothing from you." He looked at Cochrane. "I have not touched this man," he said. "If you will turn to face your peers." Cochrane wanted to flee, to be anywhere except at the center of attention. Having no agency to act, except by command of the Indian, he turned. The Indian reached over Cochrane's shoulders, grabbed the lapels of his coat, and yanked it open. "Behold, he is covered in blood!" The crowd gasped. "Like Macbeth, he cannot wash his hands of his evil deed!"

Cochrane half-turned, looked at the Indian. "What's this? You devil!"

"A simple trick," called a man from the audience. "A plant. An associate of yours. Did he not spill dye on himself just moments ago, while our attention was directed at you?"

The crowd looked to the speaker, to Cochrane, to the Indian. The Indian set Cochrane's coat back in place. "Ah, the skeptical mind of the Westerner," he said. "If you will step forth, sir." The Indian kept a tight grip on Cochrane's shoulder, arresting escape. The skeptical man stepped up. The Indian looked down at him. "You are, of course, wise to suspect me." The man looked to his friends and smiled. The Indian looked to Cochrane. "If this man is guilty, if he speaks with the serpent's tongue, if he has *not* come from a performance, as he claims, but from the scene of a murder, the murder of his own father, no less, if he has been the instrument of Death, if he wears his father's blood, should not his heart be black and lifeless?" The Indian's tone was a challenge. He returned his gaze to the skeptic, who looked up at him. "Take his wrist," commanded the Indian. "Feel for a pulse, you'll find none."

The man looked at Cochrane, hesitating. It was against proper etiquette to grab another man without his invitation, yet the circumstances called for it. Cochrane said nothing. He knew he had a pulse and saw a way out of his bind. The man reached out, took Cochrane's wrist between his fingers, and began a search. He looked to the Indian. "Some trick," he said. "He has some deformity, a blockage, a sunken vein."

"Are you able to find a pulse?" asked the Indian.

"No."

"What?" said Cochrane.

The man looked to him. "If you will permit me?" The man's gaze darted to Cochrane's neck.

"Do as you must," said the Indian.

Cochrane, again, said nothing.

The man began to feel along Cochrane's neck. This second search was as fruitless as the first. He looked into Cochrane's eyes, to the audience, to the Indian. "This man has no pulse."

"Are *you* a plant, sir?" asked the Indian. "An associate of mine?"

The man shook his head, then backed away from Cochrane. The Indian released Cochrane's shoulder. He clapped his hands together and laughed. "What do your sciences say about this?" Cochrane lifted a hand to his neck. "In my country this man's condition would be understood. Perhaps, on account of his crime, he has been cursed by the gods." The Indian looked to Cochrane. The shape of his brow condemning. Cochrane dropped his hand to his side. The Indian looked back to the audience. "Or, perhaps, I, being a magi, have used magic to match this man's heart with his actions." The Indian allowed a dramatic pause. "Of course, we are not in my country." He held out his hands. "Perhaps, this has been an elaborate trick. Perhaps, sir," he nodded to the skeptic, "I have found an assistant who is both adept at sleight-of-hand and also capable of regulating the functions of his circulatory system. Such a man would be rare, but his existence accounts for all the facts." He paused again.

"You see, my ultimate lesson is this, you have witnessed something fantastic this evening. Something that cannot be illuminated with the light of reason. How then, when reason fails, will you explain this mystery? What came before reason? Superstition? Fear? Or was this magic? That ancient law. You will wrap this display in some construct. The rational mind never fails to rationalize. Ask yourself, though, will your explanation be the truth?" The Indian bowed his head and folded his hands.

For a moment the audience was silent. Once the queer display was accepted, they broke out into enthusiastic applause. Several men stepped forward and examined Cochrane's clothing. Was it blood or was it dye? There was a desire to feel for his pulse, to verify, but such rude behavior was checked by common decency and civility. Still, the men looked suspiciously at him, the women, not at all. The Indian stepped down from the stage, disappearing among the mass of bodies. Cochrane, finally free from the other man's grip, both physical and force of will, fled for the second time that evening. He rushed away from the door, looking back to see if he was being followed.

"You are going my way."

Cochrane spun. The Indian stood before him. For a moment Cochrane saw him not as he had been in the parlor, a man, although foreign, still a man. He saw him altogether differently, as something inhuman, even fantastical.

The Indian was taller, more robust. His musculature stretched the fabric of his suit. His hands were differently shaped, no longer the familiar palm, fingers, and thumb, but paws, black-furred, the fingers capped by claws. Cochrane lifted his gaze and found himself looking not into the Indian's white eyes, but into the eyes of a panther. The black beard had become fur, human features had transmogrified into those of a cat. Golden eyes marked Cochrane's growing horror. Lips rose, a pink tongue, populated with white spines, tools for ripping flesh, curled past the blood-stained teeth, combed the short fur above the lips, arranging the whiskers, then retreated back into the humid cave of the mouth.

Cochrane blinked. The image was gone. He was stunned. He forced himself to study the other man, to see him *as* a man, and only a man. Certainly, he reasoned, the foreigner was nothing more. This gave him a temporary courage. "The hell I am!"

"If they see us walking together," said the Indian, "they will believe we are indeed associates. They will construct an interpretation that says they were skillfully tricked." The Indian looked to Cochrane. "Such a belief would be better than the truth, don't you agree?" The Indian turned and began up the sidewalk. Cochrane followed.

"The truth?" he asked, his tone sharp, defensive, demanding of proof.

The Indian gave none.

"You played me wrong in there," said Cochrane. "You're nothing but a charlatan."

The Indian continued up the hill, having made no acknowledgment of Cochrane's speech. The pair, although enveloped in café chatter, maintained an uncomfortable silence. The tension grew too great for Cochrane to bear. His mind began to question what it was he'd seen. A devil? A beast? A phantasm brought into being by his emotional state? Some trick whose workings were unknown? Beyond that, what did the other man know? The Indian had accused him of murder. Had he seen the blood when Cochrane first entered the room? Upon seeing it, had he seized the opportunity it presented, constructing a narrative that would shock his audience and make a better trick than the one he'd planned?

But patricide? Why did he say patricide? How could he— No. It was a guess. He's fishing.

Cochrane leaned into the Indian. "Blackmail, that's what you're after," he said. "You saw wine spilled on my shirt and your thieving mind constructed some fantasy. You think I—"

The Indian reached out, grabbed Cochrane's arm, and pulled him to a stop. Cochrane turned his head, looked at the other man, whose face had resumed that horrific construction. The rakshasa's panther eyes began to glow with an inner light.

Cochrane watched as the rakshasa levitated, then rotated forward, as if on a central axis. The paw's grip lessened, then fell away. At the same time he spun, turning so that he now faced Cochrane, now faced the naked sky. He began to move around Cochrane. He floated before Cochrane, face up, his whiskers and wet nose catching the moonlight, his feet at Cochrane's waist, his body extending away, as if he lie on a plank.

Cochrane stared in disbelief. He looked around him. In the distance, people drank and laughed, incapable, it seemed, of acting as witnesses to the unreal predicament he was in. Cochrane returned his attention to the fantastic.

"Babruvahana," said the rakshasa, "killed his father, Arjun." The rakshasa breathed in and out with heavy, labored breaths, taxed by his efforts to violate natural law. "Apsu was killed by his son, Ea."

"What are you saying?" asked Cochrane. "Damn you! How could you know?"

The rakshasa tilted his head forward. He curled his lips, his fangs locked together. He issued a low growl. He tilted his head back, his glowing, golden eyes gazing at the stars above. He moved now as if a hinge were at his heels.

The rakshasa appeared to be turning upright. When Cochrane saw the road fall away, saw the hill tumble out of view, when he saw the buildings pivot, moving away from him, saw the cornices of the buildings he had just passed come into view, followed by sky and stars, he realized that it was not the rakshasa alone who violated nature's laws. He felt the hard, impenetrable surface of the sidewalk at his back. He felt the back of his skull rest on it. The rakshasa now stood on top of him.

"Like Zeus, and his father before him, you've destroyed the one who created you," said the rakshasa, looking down at him. "Is that not your father's blood on your jacket? Does not your father's blood stain your soul?"

Cochrane felt the sidewalk soften. It became a thick quilt that accepted him. The rakshasa's weight pushed him into the earth. "How could I know?" He grinned, a predator's smile. "Your father's blood called out to me."

"I—" Cochrane could no longer speak. His mouth filled with sand and soil. He saw neither sky nor star, saw no longer a man wearing a panther's face, or anything else. He had been interred.

"In my travels," he heard the rakshasa say, his voice muffled, "I often come across other *evil* spirits." He laughed, the sound reverberating in the earth encasing Cochrane. The joviality left the rakshasa's voice, replaced by malice. "I show them no mercy."

Cochrane felt more then heard the footfalls of the Indian as he passed overhead.

H. Rad Bethlen has been compared to Isak Dinesen (*Seven Gothic Tales*) and Fritz Leiber (*Swords and Deviltry*). He is known for his work in the fantasy and horror genres as well as his non-fiction. He has been published in Europe and America.

Enjoy these stories?

If you liked what you read, please take a moment to **leave a review on Amazon**! Your feedback helps other readers find these stories. It only takes a minute but it makes a huge difference. The Amazon algorithm requires 30-50 reviews before it will pick this book up and promote it to like-minded readers. Your review is instrumental in helping that happen!

For more great fiction and non-fiction please visit:

roosterandravenpublishing.com

hradbethlen.com

or H. Rad Bethlen's Amazon page.

www.ingramcontent.com/pod-product-compliance
Lightning Source LLC
Chambersburg PA
CBHW071217130626
46555CB00004B/1748